The Queen and the Coffee Bear

by Lindsay Andreotti

Illustrations by Julie Hartley

HARA
PUBLISHING GROUP

**Published by
Hara Publishing
P.O. Box 19732
Seattle, WA 98109**

**To order additional copies of this book,
please contact Hara Publishing at 1-800-461-1931.**

**To contact the author and illustrator,
please send email to storia@earthlink.net**

ISBN: 1-883697-66-2

10 9 8 7 6 5 4 3 2

Illustrations: Julie Hartley
Cover Design: Scott Fisher and Julie Hartley
Book Design & Production: Scott and Shirley Fisher

Printed in Korea

Dedications

This book is dedicated to my prince Joe, my dear family, and my amazing friends. For without their love and support, my creativity could not soar.

--Lindsay

Thanks to Sean and Lucky, my two biggest fans.

--Julie

i

The Queen and the Coffee Bear

1

Way way back,
a long time ago,
lived a lovely old queen
and her brave son, prince Joe.

They reigned in a town
where it rained quite a lot
it was cold, gray, and cloudy
more often than not.

3

The townsfolk were happy
in spite of the rain
'til one day one winter
an idea came.

"We need some way
to warm us all up
something we could carry
around in a cup.

It needs to be portable
so we can still move about.
It can not hurt our environment.
It can not make people pout.

It needs to be something
that will warm us inside.
It can not be costly,
so no one's denied."

5

So the queen hearing this
proclaimed that same day,
"Let the search for our warmer
begin right away!"

"The man, woman or child
who can find the town warmer
will be rewarded handsomely;
we'll put their name on the corner."

7

8

So the brave townsfolk set out,
including Prince Joe
to find the town warmer
But where did they go?

Some folks made their way
to neighboring towns
seeking ideas that could
warm their friends up and down.

While the townsfolk stayed local
to seek out the solution,
Prince Joe stocked a ship
and set sail on the ocean.

The seas were quite rough
For twenty three days.
The brave prince and his crew
Sailed through a wave maze.

They were confused and bewildered
When they finally reached land.
They saw bright sun and palm trees
As their toes hit the sand.

12

Nothing at first glance
Met their needs for a warmer,
So they packed up, went exploring
When they met a kind farmer.

They rode on a yak
And fell down in deep ruts.
As the farmer led Joe
To a village of huts.

13

14

They crossed over a canyon,
Trudged through a ravine
When they gazed up at the most
Wonderful hillside of green.

Red berries and broad leaves
defined these great plants.
The crew stowed a few branches
In the pockets of their pants.

Prince Joe and his crew
Grew weary and tired,
So they returned to their ship
With the plants they admired.

It was the villagers who showed them
What they had found.
They had no idea, one little bean
could be so profound.

18

The Prince traveled far
How far? We're not sure.
But he returned to Raintown
With some great news to share.

Prince Joe had discovered
the perfect creation,
in Costa Rica,
a Central American nation.

19

What he found was a bean
that by itself was not great
but when roasted and ground
a fine drink it did make.

Prince Joe shared his bean-drink
with each person he saw.
He shared it with mom,
and the Queen was in awe.

21

This drink they could carry
around in a cup.
It was inexpensive, quite warm
and cheered everyone up.

This warmer was perfect.
It met all the criteria.
It was found throughout town,
even the school cafeteria.

The Queen proclaimed the bean drink
the official town warmer.
They called the drink coffee--
and put its name on the corner.

23

The Raintown's folk were happy
And wouldn't you know,
It's the best town in the world
to get a great cup of joe!

About the Authors

Since the time they were old enough to walk, talk and draw, this northwest native team Lindsay Andreotti and Julie Hartley have been sharing adventures and stories together. The Queen and the Coffee Bean is the first published work of this 30-something creative pair who wanted to bring to life a whimsical story that both adults and kids could enjoy. Lindsay is a mentor and a muse with her own management consulting company, Storia, Inc. Julie is a professional artist with her own custom invitation and card company. Brimming with creativity and passion, watch for future adventures these two bring to life!

28